Seedling Exams

Bimi

Twink

Pix

Sooze

Sili

Zena

Mariella

Lola

Glitterwings Academy

Book Eight

Seedling Exams

Titania Woods

Illustrated by Smiljana Coh

BLOOMSBURY
CHILDREN'S
BOOKS

First published in Great Britain in 2008 by Bloomsbury Publishing Plc
36 Soho Square, London, W1D 3QY

A CIP catalogue record of this book is available from the British Library

ISBN 978 0 7475 9203 7

All papers used by Bloomsbury Publishing are natural, recyclable products made
from wood grown in well-managed forests. The manufacturing processes conform to
the environmental regulations of the country of origin.

Typeset by Dorchester Typesetting Group Ltd
Printed in Singapore by Tien Wah Press

1 3 5 7 9 10 8 6 4 2

www.glitterwingsacademy.co.uk

For Mrs Boswell – teacher extraordinaire

Chapter One

Twink Flutterby's heart quickened as she and her parents crested the icy hill. Any moment now . . . any moment . . . and then all at once, there it was! Glitterwings Academy, its bare branches sparkling with frost in the winter sunshine.

Hurrah, good old Glitterwings! thought Twink. Even if this term wasn't going to be the easiest, she was still pleased to be back.

'Oh, isn't it lovely this time of year!' breathed Twink's mother. Twink's father chuckled, and he and Twink exchanged an amused glance. Twink's mother

always thought her old school looked wonderful, no matter what the season.

But she was right, thought Twink as they swooped to land on the frozen front lawn, where crowds of returning students were milling about with their parents. Her school *was* the most beautiful in the world!

Glitterwings Academy was located inside a massive oak tree on a hill. Tiny golden windows wound their way up its trunk, and a set of grand double doors sat at its base. Glancing upwards, Twink picked out Peony Branch, where she and her friends had lived for the past three terms. Excitement darted through her. She could hardly wait to see everyone again!

Miss Shimmery, the HeadFairy, flew forward to greet them, her rainbow wings gleaming like icicles. 'Twink, welcome back! Are you ready for the Seedling Exams?'

Twink's stomach tightened abruptly at the thought of the important exams waiting for her at the end of the term. 'I – I think so,' she said, trying to smile.

'I'm sure you'll do well.' Miss Shimmery's blue eyes were kind. 'It's Creature Kindness you're especially interested in, isn't it?'

'That's right,' put in Twink's father proudly. 'She wants to be a Fairy Medic, just like her parents.'

An embarrassed flush lit Twink's cheeks. 'Dad!' she hissed. It was true that being a Fairy Medic was all she'd ever wanted to do, but he didn't have to *tell* everyone!

Miss Shimmery laughed. 'Well, I'm sure you'll make a splendid medic. Have a good term, Twink – and don't worry, you'll do fine.' She flitted off in a flash of snowy-white hair.

Miss Sparkle, the dour second-year head, was standing on one of the tree's frosted roots, checking in her students. Once Twink had been ticked off the list, her father handed her her oak-leaf bag.

'Don't worry about the exams. Just do your best, Twinkster,' he said, gently ruffling her long pink hair. 'That's all we want.'

'We'll be proud of you no matter how you do,

darling,' her mother assured her with a hug. 'We know you'll try hard.'

Twink waved as her parents flew off, watching until they disappeared over the hill. Then she dropped her arm with a sigh. Her mum and dad might *say* they didn't mind if she didn't do well in her exams . . . but deep down, Twink knew they'd be disappointed. They were so pleased that she wanted to follow in their wing strokes!

'Twink!' cried a voice.

Twink spun about and saw Bimi Bluebell, her best friend, flying rapidly towards her. The two fairies met with an excited hug, wings fluttering. 'I'm so glad to see you!' said Twink.

'Me too,' said Bimi, pushing back a strand of dark blue hair. 'Oh, but Twink, I'm so nervous! I can't believe we have the Seedlings this term!'

Twink felt a rush of sympathy for Bimi. She wasn't at all confident in her studies, and was even more nervous about the exams than Twink.

'You'll do fine,' she said, rubbing her lavender wing against Bimi's silver and gold one. 'You just

need to have more faith in yourself.'

'I suppose so,' said Bimi, screwing up her face. 'Anyway, let's not think about it yet. Come on, let's go and grab our beds!' Picking up their bags, they skimmed towards the school, darting around clusters of hovering, chatting students.

As they swooped through the open front doors, Twink gazed happily around her. She never grew tired of this inside view of her school: a high, golden tower, with branches leading off in all directions. Fairies swooped in and out of these like brightly coloured birds.

The two friends spiralled upwards until they came to a branch at the top of the school, with a large pink flower hanging over its ledge. Twink sighed as they touched down. 'I can't believe it's our last term in Peony Branch. I'm really going to miss it!'

Bimi nodded. 'I know, but I'm sure we'll love our new branch, too.' They pushed open the door and flitted inside.

Maybe Bimi was right, thought Twink, but no branch could ever be prettier than this. Peony

Branch was a gently curving space lined with cosy moss beds, each with a peony blossom overhead like a frilly pink canopy. Glow-worm lanterns dangled from the ceiling, casting a warm light.

A few of the others had already arrived, and were unpacking their things.

'Opposite!' cried a voice. Sooze, a fairy with lavender hair and pink wings – the exact *opposite* to Twink – skimmed across the branch and caught Twink up in a hug. 'Hurrah, you're here!'

'Hi, Sooze,' said Twink with a grin. She and Sooze had been best friends once, and were still close – though Twink knew she had the best friend ever in Bimi now.

'Hello, you two!' called Pix cheerfully from across the branch. 'Are you ready for the Seedlings?'

Sooze's smile faded. 'That's all you've talked about since you got here,' she snapped at Pix. 'Some of us aren't looking forward to them, you know!'

Her voice wavered slightly, and Twink grimaced in understanding. The term before, Sooze had been caught setting off fairy dust flares, and as punishment she wasn't allowed to use fairy dust at all this term – not even for her Fairy Dust practical. As a result, she was going to have to work extremely hard to move up to the third year.

'Well, you're not alone – I'm not looking forward to them, either,' confessed Twink.

'But *you* won't be fifty points down to start with,' pointed out Sooze, her expression glum. 'I might as well not even bother.'

'Yes, that's too bad,' said Bimi stiffly.

Twink knew her best friend still hadn't forgiven Sooze for accidentally singeing off her hair with the flares – though it had all grown back now, and was just as beautiful as before.

Catching Bimi's tone, Sooze made a face. 'All right, I'm sorry *again*,' she said. 'But I'm paying the price now, aren't I?'

'You'll do all right if you try, Sooze,' said Pix earnestly. 'You've just got to take it seriously, and work hard.'

'Well, I don't know why everyone's getting so worked up,' sniffed a pointy-faced fairy called

Mariella. 'They're only exams! Besides,' she added with a smirk, 'my mum says they wouldn't dare hold any of us back, or else it would look bad on *them*.'

'Don't you believe it,' said Sooze shortly. 'They would, all right!'

'Ooh, I'm all nervous now,' exclaimed an excitable fairy called Sili. She pushed back her bright silver hair. 'Can't we talk about something else? How were everyone's hols?'

As the rest of the branch started talking, Twink

and Bimi flitted to their favourite beds at the end of the row, which the others had left free for them. Bimi shook her head as they started to unpack.

'It doesn't seem like it's going to be a very fun term, does it?' she murmured.

Twink placed a drawing of her family on her bedside mushroom, adjusting it carefully. 'No . . . I don't think *fun* is quite the word.' Then she smiled. 'It's still good to be back, though.'

Later, their belongings all put away, the Peony Branch fairies flew down to the Great Branch: a long, gleaming space lined with mossy tables and overhanging flowers. Twink fidgeted as Miss Shimmery hovered above the platform, making the usual start-of-term announcements: no high-speed flying in the school, uniforms required from the next day, no bothering the water sprites in the pond . . .

We know *all of this!* thought Twink. When were they going to find out more about their Seedling Exams? Then she sat up, her heart thumping. Miss

Shimmery was looking towards the second-year tables!

'Finally, may I request that the second-year students stay behind after dinner, so that Miss Sparkle can go over the Seedling Exams with them,' said the HeadFairy in her strong, low voice. 'That's all – I hope you all have a wonderful term!' She drifted back down to the platform.

Sooze groaned as conversation broke out across the Branch. 'Oh, wasps! How are we supposed to eat with *that* hanging over us?'

'Sooze, that's not the right attitude,' chided Pix, tapping her yellow wings together. 'I know you've got a tough term ahead, but if you just try to look on it as a learning opportunity –'

Just then the Great Branch's doors swung open. In a bright rainbow of wings, the school's butterflies floated in, carrying oak-leaf platters piled high with seed cakes and nectar. A yellow and white butterfly served the Peony table, waving its antennae in a friendly hello.

'Hurrah, saved by the butterflies!' said Sooze with

a grin. 'You were saying, Pix?'

'Never mind!' groaned Pix. 'You're hopeless, Sooze.'

Finally dinner was over, and the rest of the school had departed. Twink thought her year group looked very small, on their own in the large Branch with so many empty tables around them.

Miss Sparkle's pale wings glinted as she bobbed in the air. 'As you know, this is an extremely important term for you,' she said. 'Your Seedling Exams will decide whether or not you move up to the third year, and which advanced subjects you'll take.'

Twink's pulse quickened. Oh, she just *had* to do well! The Seedling Exams were her first step towards becoming a Fairy Medic.

'The exams for each of your five subjects will consist of both a practical and a written exam, each worth fifty points,' their year head went on. 'You must score at *least* three hundred and fifty points to move up into the third year.'

The second-year fairies hardly moved as they gazed back at her, wide-eyed and solemn. Bimi swallowed hard, and clutched Twink's hand. Across the table, Sooze looked quite pale.

'If you wish to go on to the advanced classes in a particular subject, then you must score at least eighty-five points in that subject.' Miss Sparkle regarded them gravely. 'The best thing, of course, is to try to do well in *all* your exams, so that you have lots of choices next year.'

Creature Kindness, thought Twink fervently. As Miss Shimmery had said, that was the subject she had to excel in to be a Fairy Medic. Nothing else mattered!

Pix raised her hand. 'When do we find out about our practicals, Miss?' Her eyes were shining in expectation. Twink and Bimi exchanged a look. Trust Pix not to be worried. She'd probably get the best marks in the year, too!

'Your practicals will be term-long projects,' explained Miss Sparkle. 'They'll be announced tomorrow. Are there any other questions?'

No one spoke, and Miss Sparkle nodded. 'You may return to your branches, then. And girls, try not to worry too much. Those of you who have been working hard all along will be at an advantage this term, but it's not too late for the rest of you. Just buckle down and study, and you'll be fine!'

After glow-worms out that night, Twink lay awake for ages in her mossy bed, gazing at the drawing of her family. Her parents' faces smiled at her in the moonlight.

For as long as she could remember, Twink had wanted to be a Fairy Medic, so she could help injured wild creatures just like her parents did. Brownie, the Flutterby family's mouse, had spent many long-suffering hours wrapped up in leafy bandages and sneezing clouds of fake fairy dust as Twink pretended to heal him.

Then, when she was older, her parents had sometimes let her come along to visit their patients: injured birds or badgers recuperating under their care, who were always smiling and happy to see them. No wonder! Everyone who knew Twink's parents knew they were the wisest, kindest fairies in the world.

I won't let them down, thought Twink firmly, closing her eyes and pulling her petal duvet around her. *I'll do well in my exams . . . no matter what!*

Chapter Two

At breakfast the next morning, the Great Branch seemed a different place from the quiet, tense room of the night before. Hundreds of fairies sat chattering at their tables, all of them resplendent in fresh flower uniforms. Sitting at the Peony Branch table with the others, Twink smoothed the pink skirt of her new dress.

'We've got Flower Power first today,' she said to Bimi. Mrs Hover, the matron, had handed out their timetables earlier that morning, when she made their peony dresses.

Bimi nodded worriedly. 'I wonder what our practical will be like?'

'I hope it's nothing to do with changing the colours of leaves,' said a lilac-haired fairy called Kiki, who had only been in their branch since the previous term. 'I'm *awful* at that!'

'Ooh, me too!' shuddered Sili. 'Maybe it'll be something easy, like making the flowers open.'

'In the wintertime?' hooted her friend Zena. 'You'd better get studying before the exam, Sili!'

Though Twink laughed with the others, she wasn't really bothered what they did in Flower Power. It was Creature Kindness *she* was dying to find out about! But to her surprise, their Flower Power practical turned out to be much more interesting than she'd expected.

'As you know, most trees have dryads: magical spirits that live within them,' explained Miss Petal later that morning. 'Flower Power specialists often work with dryads if we're healing a poorly tree. It's important that you learn how to contact them, and that's what you'll be doing for your practical.'

Twink and Bimi looked at each other in surprise. Contacting a dryad sounded like a lot more fun than perking up drooping daisies or making the grass greener!

'But Miss Petal, how do we do *that?*' breathed Sili, wide-eyed.

The attractive young teacher smiled. 'The best way is to sit beside a tree and try talking to its dryad in your mind. If the dryad likes the look of you, he or she will respond.'

'Hurrah, an easy practical!' whispered Sooze, her violet eyes dancing.

Miss Petal raised an amused eyebrow. 'It's not as easy as it sounds, Sooze – that's why you've got a whole term! You have to make yourself seem likeable to the dryads, or else they'll just ignore you.'

'Likeable? What do you mean?' asked Mariella, wrinkling up her forehead.

Twink glanced at Sooze. Normally her Opposite wouldn't have been able to resist a joke at the haughty fairy's expense, but now she just sat anxiously with the others, waiting for the answer.

Miss Petal considered, cocking her head to one side. 'It's difficult to explain,' she said finally. 'I suppose it's all to do with having the right mindset. You have to imagine what it's like to be part of a tree, and go on from there.'

The fairies stared at each other. This was sounding harder and harder! Twink stifled a nervous giggle as she pictured herself with roots growing out of her pixie boots, and leafy branches sprouting from her head.

Miss Petal

Pix raised her hand. 'Miss Petal, is it true that the older a dryad gets, the harder they are to contact?'

'You've been reading up as usual, haven't you, Pix?' smiled Miss Petal. 'Yes, that's right. After a few centuries, dryads almost go to sleep and can be very difficult to rouse. So the best bet for your practical is to choose a young tree to talk to.'

Opening her petal pad, Twink wrote *Choose a young tree* with her snail-trail pen. Excitement tickled her wings. Contacting a dryad sounded like glimmery fun – if she was able to do it!

'You'll want to start trying to make contact with a dryad very soon, so you can show me on the day that you're able to speak to one,' concluded Miss Petal. 'Try the wood; there are lots of likely trees there. And good luck!' She raised her voice as the magpie's screech echoed through the school, signalling the end of the lesson.

Their other practicals sounded interesting as well, though not terribly easy. In Weather Magic they had to create a flurry of snowflakes, while in Dance they were to learn a complicated dance that sent pleasant dreams to hibernating creatures. Even trickier was Fairy Dust, where they had to master the spell that changed a flower into a petal dress.

When it was finally time for Creature Kindness, Twink was in a daze. There was so much to do! How was she ever going to manage it all? The others looked just as worried. Even Pix had a concerned frown on her face.

'Creature Kindness is in the animal infirmary this afternoon,' said Zena as they left the Fairy Dust branch. 'I saw a notice on Mr Woodleaf's door.'

The infirmary! All at once Twink's spirits soared. Working with poorly animals was just what she had hoped for.

'Come on, let's hurry!' She plunged into a dive down the trunk.

'Oh, don't look so keen,' grumbled Sooze as she followed. 'You know he'll give us *minus* fifty points if we do anything to upset his precious animals!'

The Peony Branch fairies swooped through the great double doors and out into the winter sunshine. Twink could see her breath as they flew to the animal infirmary: a large hollow log near the school pond, with cheerful windows down its side. Mr Woodleaf met them at the door.

'Ah . . . hello, girls,' he muttered. 'Come this way, please.'

Twink stared around her as they followed him. The infirmary was filled with different-sized chambers, each with a comfy nest or bed. A poorly-looking rat blinked at her from one, and a chaffinch with a bandaged foot slept in another.

Mr Woodleaf stopped in the centre of the log. As always, he seemed much more relaxed in the presence of animals, and even managed to smile at them. 'Now then – you know that fairy magic can be used to heal injured creatures. However, some creatures take longer to recover than others.'

Twink nodded. She had always felt terribly sorry for those animals that couldn't be cured quickly.

'All the patients in this infirmary are what we call *slow healers*,' continued Mr Woodleaf. 'Magic has been performed to help them get better, but it will still take a long time for them to recover fully – and to do so, they need good nursing!'

He motioned to the injured creatures. 'I'm going to assign each of you to a patient. Your practical will be to take care of it – feed and water it, change its bandages, and keep its spirits up. To pass the practical at the end of term, you'll need to show me that you can work well with your animal.'

Twink caught her breath. Oh, how glimmery! She glanced eagerly around her, wondering which animal would be hers – the mouse with the broken tail, maybe, or the glum-looking blue tit.

'Now, Bimi, I'd like you to take care of this dormouse,' said Mr Woodleaf, indicating a young dormouse with a splint on one leg. He flew to its nest and beckoned Bimi forward. With an excited glance at Twink, Bimi followed him.

'Just wait here until I've assigned everyone, please. Sooze, I'd like you to take care of this cricket . . .'

Twink stood fidgeting as the other fairies were assigned their animals one by one. Mariella got the rat; Sili, the chaffinch; Pix, the blue and yellow tit.

Oh, I hope I get the mouse! thought Twink. He had

such gentle brown eyes and sleek whiskers. And the poor thing looked so sad! She'd love to be his friend and cheer him up.

'Kiki, you're to take care of this mouse,' instructed Mr Woodleaf. 'And Zena, I'd like you to be with the mole . . .'

Oh. Twink bit her lip. But . . . what was left, in that case?

'Now, Twink.' Mr Woodleaf flitted back to her. 'I'd like you to take care of this animal over here – he's a bit apart from the others.'

Puzzled, Twink followed Mr Woodleaf to the end of the log, where there was a slight alcove. She stopped short, her eyes widening.

In the alcove was a nest with a starling in it: a great, hulking bird with untidy speckled brown feathers and a sharp black beak. One of its wings was bound up in a leafy bandage; the other flapped restlessly. Its dark, beady eyes narrowed when it saw her.

Mr Woodleaf smiled. 'Since you nursed that wasp last year, I thought you'd like something a bit more

challenging,' he explained. 'Starlings can be a bit bad-tempered, but I'm sure it's nothing you can't handle.'

'Oh,' said Twink faintly. It was true that she'd taken care of a wasp called Stripe when she was a first-year student – but *he* had been friendly! This bird was scowling at her as though he hated her already.

Swallowing hard, Twink put what she hoped was a

keen look on her face. 'Thank you, sir. I'd love to take care of him.'

'Excellent!' beamed Mr Woodleaf. 'I'm sure you'll do a splendid job.'

He flew back to the centre of the log. 'Now then!' he called, clapping his hands. 'I'd like you all to spend a bit of time getting to know your animals. Why not give them a drink of water and say hello?'

Twink slowly picked up a walnut-shell bucket full of water that sat on the floor. She could hear the others murmuring friendly greetings to their animals, and the sound of responding squeaks and chirrups.

'Um . . . would you like some water?' she asked the starling.

The bird glared at her.

Twink took a deep breath and flew forward. 'Nice starling,' she soothed. 'That's right, you're a nice starling.'

The bird looked as if he knew she was lying. '*Squuaawwk,*' he cawed.

Twink stopped in front of his nest, her pulse thudding as she hovered. She held out the bucket. 'Here you are,' she said nervously. 'Nice water for the nice starling!'

Without warning, the bird's beak dived into the bucket. He drank greedily, with loud slurping noises. Twink winced as drops of water flew everywhere, splattering her arms.

Finally the starling raised his head, smacking his beak.

Twink tried to smile. 'Hello!' she said. 'I'm Twink. I'm going to be taking care of you.'

The bird rustled his feathers grumpily and turned away.

Twink bit her lip. Glancing over her shoulder, she could see Bimi sitting beside her dormouse, and Sili stroking her chaffinch's head. They all looked like they were getting on really well already!

Shifting the bucket to one hand, Twink flitted a bit closer. 'I'm sure we'll be good friends,' she said hopefully. Very softly, she reached out and stroked the starling's good wing.

'SQUAAWWKK!'

The bird exploded into a series of outraged shrieks and wing-flappings that sent Twink and the bucket flying. Suddenly she found herself sprawled on the floor several wingspans away, with her pink hair drenched and the bucket lying upside-down beside her.

Mr Woodleaf hurried over. 'Twink! What happened?'

Water dripped off Twink's dress as he helped her up. Behind her, the bird was still screeching indignantly. Twink's cheeks felt on fire. She could see the others all staring at her in concern – except for Mariella, who had an amused smirk on her face!

'I'm fine,' she said quickly, though one of her wings was throbbing. 'I startled him a bit, that's all! And . . . then I fell over.' She *couldn't* let Mr Woodleaf know that she was having problems already – this was her most important practical!

'Oh, I see,' said her teacher. 'Well, be sure to move more slowly around him next time, until he gets used to you.'

Twink nodded vigorously, and Mr Woodleaf left her alone with the starling again. She and the bird looked at each other. He had stopped squawking, but was still glaring at her, his speckled feathers ruffled ominously.

Twink sighed. She could tell already that it was going to be a very long term.

Chapter Three

'Dear, oh dear!' Mrs Hover shook her bright pink head. 'That *is* a nasty bruise. How did you say you did it again?'

'I, um – fell over,' mumbled Twink, feeling hot. She sat perched on one of the mossy beds in the infirmary as the matron rubbed arrowroot salve on her sore wing.

Saying a quick spell over a pinch of fairy dust, Mrs Hover sprinkled it over the injury. Immediately, the harsh throbbing stopped. 'There you are, dear – is that better?' she asked cheerfully.

Twink stretched her wing, glancing over her shoulder at it. 'Yes, much, Mrs Hover – thanks!' she said in relief. She hopped off the bed.

'Not at all,' said Mrs Hover, putting away the fairy dust. 'Now, you take it easy for a few days. No high-speed flying for you, my girl!'

'No, I won't,' said Twink. She hesitated, biting her lip. 'Um, Mrs Hover . . . what would you do if – if you had a patient who didn't like you? I mean – who didn't like *anyone*?'

Mrs Hover looked surprised. 'Well, I'm glad to

say that such patients are few and far between! All of my Glitterwings girls are lovely.'

'But if you *did*,' pressed Twink.

Mrs Hover's plump face creased in thought. 'I'd just have to be patient, I suppose. So long as you're kind and consistent, most folk will come around.'

'Consistent?' asked Twink anxiously.

Mrs Hover nodded, smoothing down the bed. 'That's right. I'd make sure that I was always very steady and kind, you see – it's no good being kind one day and snappish the next! Patients have to know that they can trust you. And most of them will, in time.'

'Oh,' murmured Twink. 'So . . . you think it just takes time?'

Mrs Hover gave her a keen look. 'Is everything all right, my dear?'

'Oh, yes!' said Twink. She smiled. 'I've got to go now, Mrs Hover – but thanks!'

Flying back to Peony Branch, Twink realised that Mrs Hover was right. It had been daft of her to try to be the starling's friend instantly – they were bad-tempered birds, like Mr Woodleaf had said. It would take time to make him like her.

'I've just got to be patient,' she muttered. She *would* win the starling over, and show Mr Woodleaf that she could work well with any animal there was! After all, animals always loved her parents . . . surely she'd inherited just a little of their skill?

After dinner the next evening, Twink and Bimi borrowed a glow-worm lantern from the supplies branch and flew down to the animal infirmary. The light from their lantern gleamed brightly on the snowy ground, showing the way.

Bimi had hardly stopped talking about her dormouse all day. 'He's *so* cute,' she enthused now as they flew along. 'And his fur's so soft! I've got a thistle comb in my bag, and I'm going to see if he'll let me groom him tonight.'

'That's a good idea,' said Twink. She hoped her smile didn't look half-hearted. She was very pleased for Bimi, but she wasn't really in the mood to hear how wonderful her dormouse was.

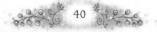

'Well, he's a bit nervous,' said Bimi thoughtfully. 'I'm hoping that he'll relax soon.'

'I'm sure he will.' Twink gazed towards the infirmary, wondering what sort of reception she was going to get from the starling. Would he be even grumpier than before?

Suddenly Bimi seemed to realise that Twink might not be feeling as eager as she was. A guilty flush lit her face. 'Oh, Twink, I'm sorry! What

about your starling? Are you nervous about seeing him again?' Twink had sheepishly told her friend what had really happened.

'A little,' she confessed as they landed. 'But I'll win him over, you'll see! This is one practical I've *got* to do well in.'

They pushed the door open. Pix was already there, and waved to them across the log.

'Look, I've got my bird eating out of my hand!' she called happily. 'You love poppy seeds, don't you?' she crooned to the blue and yellow bird, reaching up to stroke its neck.

'Great,' said Twink, forcing a smile. She glanced down the length of the infirmary. The alcove hid the starling from her, but she knew he was in there, crouched in his untidy nest.

Not wanting to admit to herself that she was stalling, Twink drifted over to Bimi's dormouse, exclaiming with her friend over his sleek fur and sensitive, twitching nose.

'He's lovely, Bimi,' she said sincerely, stroking his round ear.

'I know.' Bimi's cheeks were pink with excitement as she combed the dormouse's fur. He sighed happily, his eyes half closing in bliss.

Finally Twink could put it off no longer. Straightening her shoulders, she flitted down the log.

The starling seemed just as grimy and ill-tempered as the day before. He stared coldly at her, looking as if he had been expecting her to come back, just to irritate him.

'Hi,' said Twink. She stretched her mouth into a cheerful smile. 'I'm sorry about yesterday. I didn't mean to startle you.'

The starling's eyes narrowed. '*Squaawwkk,*' he said. It didn't sound like an apology.

'Are you thirsty?' asked Twink. 'Or would you like something to eat?'

The bird accepted both food and water, but hardly looked at Twink as his beak pecked at the buckets. When he had finished, he glared at her and tucked his head under his good wing.

Kind and consistent! thought Twink. 'Why don't I

sing you to sleep?' she suggested. The bird didn't respond. Clearing her throat, Twink began to sing a soft fairy lullaby.

> *'Fluttering fairy,*
> *Been flying so long,*
> *When the moon shows,*
> *It's time for this song.*
> *Your mossy bed's calling,*
> *Your wings feeling tired,*
> *Come creep into bed,*
> *For it's time to – oh!'*

Twink darted backwards as the bird swiped at her with his good wing, only just missing her this time. With a pointed stare, he shuffled about in his nest so that his back was to her, and shoved his head under his wing again.

Twink bit her lip. 'I . . . suppose you don't like music, then.'

The bird ignored her. Twink gathered up the food and water buckets with a sigh. Never mind, she thought. It was going to take time, that was all. She'd just have to try again tomorrow.

But the next day came, and was no different – and the next day, and the next. After a week with no success, Twink flew glumly to the wood one afternoon to work on her Flower Power practical. It wasn't easy to put Creature Kindness out of her head, but she knew she had to – or else she wouldn't pass any of her other practicals, either!

'Choose a young tree,' she murmured, looking around her. There, that one would do: a slender birch sapling with slim, snowy-white branches.

She leaned against its trunk and frowned uncertainly. Imagine being part of the tree, Miss Petal had said – but how did you do that? She took a deep breath and closed her eyes.

I'm part of the tree, she thought. *Part of the tree . . .*

The world around her seemed to fade. Twink pictured herself inside the tree's roots, plunging deep into the ground. Then she was going upwards, flowing with the sap that moved through the tree's trunk and limbs. Finally she became its branches, reaching up towards the grey sky . . .

Hello! said a friendly voice in her mind. An image of a tall, slim girl dressed in shimmering white popped into Twink's head.

'Oh!' gasped Twink, her eyes flying open.

What's wrong? Don't you want to talk to me? asked the girl.

Um . . . yes! thought Twink in a daze. *Are you the tree's dryad?*

Of course! laughed the girl. *I'm called Sheena. Who are you?*

I'm Twink Flutterby, thought Twink. *I go to school at Glitterwings Academy.*

Her heart was thumping so hard that she barely heard Sheena's response. She was actually talking with a dryad – a real dryad! And she could see her so clearly: a snowy-pale, slender girl with shining green eyes and long leafy hair.

I'm glad I don't have to go to school, giggled Sheena, propping her chin on her hand. *Being a dryad is much more fun!*

Oh, but school can be fun, too, answered Twink eagerly. *We do all sorts of things.*

She and the dryad chatted for ages. Twink learned that Sheena was three years old, and that she loved to feel the moonlight on her hair. Sheena, in turn, was fascinated by Twink's description of her family and home.

Finally Twink glanced at the setting sun, and realised with a start what time it was. *I've got to go!* she thought, jumping up. *It's been glimmery talking to you, Sheena.*

Come and visit me again, said Sheena, blowing her a kiss from a pale hand.

I will! promised Twink. She skimmed back to school with a wide grin on her face. Well, at least that was *one* practical she had sorted!

Chapter Four

'Not bad,' said Miss Sparkle, surveying Twink's latest effort: a rose dress with one sleeve longer than the other.

Twink smiled ruefully. 'I wouldn't want to wear it, though.' She tossed a pinch of fairy dust on the dress. With a shimmer of pink and gold, it changed back into a rosebud.

'Look at *mine*,' groaned Bimi, holding up a lopsided blue dress. 'But I suppose it's better than last time,' she added. 'That one didn't even have any wing openings!'

Miss Sparkle gave them one of her dry smiles. 'Just keep practising, girls. You'll get there.'

She moved across the branch, stopping to examine Kiki's work. 'Very good!' she exclaimed, holding up a bright purple dress with pink sleeves. 'But then, you knew this spell already, didn't you?'

Kiki nodded. 'I learned it from my mother. But it's still fun to practise; I've worked out all sorts of new things this term.'

Twink gazed at the dress in admiration. Kiki was *so* clever at this sort of thing. She'd even made all the dresses for the second-year fashion show the term before – including a truly unique one for Twink that she'd hated at first!

'Well done,' said Miss Sparkle, handing Kiki her dress back. Then she shook her head as she caught sight of Mariella's dress: a drooping, sad-looking thing with bits of petal falling off it.

'You really must work harder, Mariella,' she scolded. 'I would have expected you to be doing much better by now!'

Mariella looked sulky. 'It's not like we have any

time this term,' she muttered, shoving the dress away.

'Well, the others are managing,' said Miss Sparkle sternly. 'I suggest you use your time a bit more wisely.' She clapped her hands. 'Class is almost over, everyone – put your things away.'

Twink closed the bark box that her fairy dust was kept in, and placed it in the classroom cupboard. Maybe she was no Kiki, but she really *had* improved, she realised. The first time she'd tried the spell, her dress had fallen to bits!

They were almost halfway through the term now, and most of Twink's other practicals were going well, too: she had finally managed to create a few drifting snowflakes in Weather Magic, and the complicated steps for Dance class were already half memorised.

Those weren't the best things, though, thought Twink as she shut the cupboard door. She felt a warm glow whenever she thought about her Flower Power practical.

In the past few weeks, Twink had returned to chat with Sheena often. She had tried other trees, too, and soon found herself having conversations with dryads of all shapes and sizes: a vain young male dryad from a chestnut tree; a gloomy pine dryad with green hair and a long face; a tall, motherly spruce dryad. There were so many of them that it made Twink's head spin!

Her smile faded as the magpie's call rang through the school. She sighed, and slung her petal bag over her shoulder.

'Is everything all right?' asked Bimi as they flitted from the branch. They joined the busy stream of fairies flying down towards the Great Branch for lunch.

Twink nodded. 'Just thinking about something, that's all.'

There was no point in going on about it; Bimi had heard it many times before. Maybe she was doing well in Flower Power, but what good was *that* going to do her? It wouldn't help her pass her Creature Kindness practical . . . and the starling still hated her.

*   *   *

'Would you like me to groom your feathers?' suggested Twink wearily. She knew already what the answer would be: a grumpy squawk, or a glare, or a wing swiped at her chest.

This time, though, the bird made no response at all. He sat crouched in his nest, staring out of the window at the nearby wood. For the first time since Twink had met him, she thought he looked sad instead of angry.

She hesitated. 'Are . . . are you homesick?' she asked finally.

The starling didn't respond. His broken wing still hung awkwardly, despite the daily care that Twink gave it. Mr Woodleaf had said it would be weeks yet before the bird was well – and had warned her that starlings got very restless when they were healing.

'They hate being cooped up indoors,' he said, shaking his head. 'They've even been known to try to leave before they can fly again. You'll have to work very hard to keep his mind off things.'

To Twink's surprise, she felt a stab of sympathy for the starling. It must be awful to be shut up inside when you were used to trees and fresh air. She started to touch his good wing, and then pulled back quickly. She wasn't going to try *that* again.

Twink cleared her throat. 'I know it's awful to feel homesick,' she said. 'But I'll be your friend, if you let me. Please?' She looked earnestly into his eyes, trying to show how sincere she was.

'*Squaawk!*' snapped the starling.

With a flap of his good wing, he knocked over the seed bucket. His beak seemed to curl in a sneer. His meaning was just as clear as if he'd said, *Starlings are only friends with other starlings! Back off!*

Tears pricked at Twink's eyes as she swept up the seeds. She'd only been trying to help! Why did he have to be so *nasty* all the time? She banged the bucket back into place, and left without saying goodbye.

'It's hopeless,' she said gloomily as she, Bimi and Sooze flew back to school. 'The term's half over, and nothing I do makes any difference!'

'He's a nightmare, all right,' said Sooze. 'I'm glad *you* got him instead of me.'

'Thanks a lot,' muttered Twink. Sooze's cricket was as cheerful a creature as the others. *Her* biggest problem was in making sure he didn't jump about before his leg was healed!

Sooze shrugged, looking tired. 'Sorry – but honestly, Opposite, what can *we* do about it? Anyway, I've got to hurry, or I'll be late for my study session. See you.' She skimmed off in a flash of pink wings, disappearing through the doors of the school.

Sooze was always studying these days, thought Twink. The lavender-haired fairy was so worried about passing her exams! She had bags under her eyes from working so hard, and hadn't laughed in ages.

With a sigh, Twink returned to her own problems. 'Bimi, you're getting on so well with your dormouse,' she said, banking to avoid a frozen spiderweb. 'Do you have any ideas about what I can do? I'll try anything!'

Her best friend didn't answer. Twink glanced at her in surprise. Bimi was flying along slowly, a

distracted frown on her face. 'Bimi? What's up?' asked Twink.

Bimi started. 'Oh – nothing! Um . . . maybe you should ask Mr Woodleaf for advice.'

They had reached the school by then. Twink hovered beside the front doors. 'But then he'd realise how badly I'm doing! I've *got* to find a way to get on with the starling by the end of term, or I won't pass the practical.'

'Oh, that's right,' said Bimi, nodding quickly. 'I don't know, then. Maybe the library?'

Twink stared at her. Somehow she had the feeling that her best friend's mind was somewhere else entirely! 'Bimi, is something wrong?'

The pretty fairy's cheeks flushed bright pink. 'No, of course not! I was just – thinking of something. I've forgotten what now,' she added hastily. 'It wasn't important.' And just like Sooze, she jetted off into school.

The Glitterwings library was a tall, arching space with towering shelves that scraped the ceiling. High overhead, fairies flitted about from shelf to shelf. Snow dropped softly on the windows.

Twink sat at one of the mushroom desks, a pile of books at her elbow. She slumped her cheek on her hand as she read.

Starlings are known to be bad-tempered birds, remarkably resistant to any sort of kindness. It is recommended that fairies leave them to themselves where possible. Tits, on the other wing, are lovely creatures, which –

Twink groaned and shoved *The Fairy's Guide to*

Woodland Friends away. Yes, starlings were bad-tempered; what a surprise! What she needed to know was how to win one over – and none of the books seemed to have any advice on that at all, though she'd spent the last few days going through every one she could find.

Twink reached for the last book in her pile: *A Compendium of Non-Magical Birds*. She flipped through it, and sighed as she started to read. Why was she bothering? It was just going to say again how bad-tempered starlings were!

Suddenly Twink sat up straight, wings tingling. She read through the entry again, her finger skimming quickly across the page.

Starlings are unfriendly birds, known to hold a grudge. While most authorities maintain that their ill temper is too ingrained to overcome, Horace Cloudwing is adamant that an offering of hazelnuts will sweeten their nature, this being a favourite treat of the bird.

'Hazelnuts,' breathed Twink, as she gazed down at the words. Oh, this was it! This might really work!

Then she looked out of the window at the snow-covered branches, and bit her lip. Where would she find some at this time of year, though? The ground outside was hard and frozen.

And was there even a hazel tree in the wood? Twink couldn't recall seeing one. Still, maybe the dryads would have some ideas . . .

Lost in thought, Twink gathered up her books and flew upwards to the Creature Kindness section. As she slotted her books back into place, she glanced down – and her eyes widened.

A fairy with silver and gold wings sat alone in a shadowy corner, surrounded by books. Bimi! But what was she doing here on her own? The two of them always studied together in the Common Branch.

Twink started to swoop down to say hello to her friend . . . but then she hesitated. Bimi really didn't look as if she wanted to be disturbed. In fact, she looked as if she were trying to hide!

Twink flew slowly from the library. *She's just studying in here where it's quiet, that's all,* she told herself doubtfully. But that didn't make sense – it was quiet in the second-year Common Branch, now that the written exams were coming up. And then Twink remembered how Bimi had got so flustered outside the school the other day.

Twink frowned as she spiralled slowly up the trunk. Something was definitely up with her best friend . . . and she had no idea what.

Chapter
Five

Twink sat on the frozen ground with her eyes closed, leaning against the trunk of a hazel tree. *Are you in there?* she thought for the hundredth time. *Please come out and talk to me! I need to ask you something!*

Though she could feel the tree clearly in her mind – the ancient roots, the trunk, the twisted branches – there was no sign of its dryad at all.

It must be a very old one, thought Twink, giving up for the moment and stretching her wings. The other dryads she'd spoken to had hardly taken any

time at all to respond, even if they hadn't been able to help her.

'A hazel tree?' Sheena's pale brow had furrowed. 'Well . . . there's a pine tree over there,' she'd said, pointing. 'And an oak there . . .'

The other dryads had been the same, and Twink realised glumly that they only knew about those trees near their own. So for the last few weeks, she'd used all of her of spare time to search for a hazel tree herself. She'd almost been ready to give up when she finally found one, deep in the heart of the wood – and now its dryad refused to talk to her!

Taking a deep breath, Twink rested against the tree and tried again. *Hello, are you there?* she called. *I need to talk to you! Please come out, it's really important!*

Oh, DO be quiet! groaned an elderly voice. The image of an old man with a long, twiggy beard popped into Twink's head. He was leaning on a knotty stick, rubbing his eyes.

Twink jerked upright. *Hello!* she cried, her wings fluttering eagerly. *I've been trying and trying to reach you!*

Yes, I know! said the old man. He banged his stick on the ground. *How am I supposed to sleep, with you wittering away?*

I'll stop as soon as you answer a question, promised Twink. *Where can I find some hazelnuts?*

Right here, of course – in about nine months! snapped the dryad. *Now go away!*

No, I need them now! said Twink. *I'm trying to make friends with a starling, you see, and –*

Starlings – hmph! Nasty birds, grumbled the old man. He seemed a bit less cross, though, and narrowed his eyes in thought. *Well, you might try one of the squirrel's winter hoards. There's one just at my base, under that root.* He pointed his stick to a curved, knobbly root.

Twink hesitated. *But won't he need them?*

The dryad gave a dry, rasping laugh, like the wind rustling through bare branches. *Not him! He always stores twice as many nuts as he needs, and then forgets where he's hidden them. You help yourself, young fairy; he won't miss them. And now, if you'll excuse me – goodnight!*

With a face-cracking yawn, the old man waved his
stick at her and vanished. Twink sat smiling for a
moment, amazed that she had actually roused the
dryad. Finally, still smiling, she flitted over to the
root and started to dig.

'Well – here they are,' said Twink.

She showed Bimi and Pix a bark platter with nine
hazelnuts arranged across it. 'What do you think?
Do they look nice?' She glanced anxiously at the

nuts. How she wished that the squirrel had hidden more than nine!

'They look wonderful!' said Pix. 'He's going to be thrilled, Twink.'

The red-haired fairy's eyes were shining. All of Peony Branch knew what an awful time Twink was having with her starling, and everyone sympathised – apart from Mariella, who wasn't getting on particularly well with her rat, either.

Twink gazed towards the starling's alcove and straightened her wings. 'So . . . here goes.'

'Good luck!' Bimi squeezed her arm, and Twink smiled gratefully at her. Regardless of whatever was bothering Bimi, Twink knew her best friend was as excited and nervous as she was.

Twink flitted down the length of the hollow log, carefully balancing the platter. When she reached the alcove she briefly shut her eyes. *Oh, please, please work!* she thought. *I've tried everything else!*

Putting a bright, welcoming smile on her face, Twink rounded the corner. 'Hello!' she said.

The starling, who had been staring restlessly out

of the window, turned and gave her a sulky look. He was obviously tired of being ill, thought Twink. She didn't blame him. She was tired of him being ill, as well!

'Look, I brought you a surprise.' She held the platter out enticingly.

The starling's eyes widened when he saw the nuts. He stared at them, and then at her.

Twink flew slowly forward, until she was hovering in front of him. 'I know how much starlings love hazelnuts, so I got you some,' she said. 'Here – would you like them?' She held the platter out, her heart pounding.

Without warning, the starling lunged at the nuts. *Peck, peck, peck!* The platter shuddered as he snapped them up, one after the other. When he had finished, he raised his head and gazed thoughtfully at her.

Twink swallowed hard. 'I really want to work well with you, like Mr Woodleaf said,' she whispered. 'Do you think we can be friends?' Hope pounded through her veins. She held her breath, not daring to say more.

The starling didn't move as he stared back at her. For a moment he looked as if he were considering it, and Twink's spirits soared . . . and then he huffed out a breath and turned his back on her.

Oh! Twink hovered in a daze, hardly able to believe it. It hadn't worked. All those weeks she had spent searching for the nuts! She had hoped so much, tried so hard . . . and none of it made any difference.

Sudden tears almost blinded her. Dropping the platter, Twink flew clumsily from the alcove. She couldn't face her friends now, she just couldn't! There was a back door to the infirmary, rarely used. Shoving it open, Twink flew away as fast as she could, skimming over the frozen grass.

As though her wings knew exactly where to take her, she flew straight to the abandoned caretaker's stump, where she had sheltered Stripe the wasp the previous year. Ducking through the weather-beaten entrance, Twink flitted to the mossy bed and flung herself on it, hugging the pillow.

It felt wonderful to cry after holding in her feelings for so long. Finally, when the pillow was damp with tears, Twink sniffed and sat up, wiping her eyes. She smiled slightly. Oh, she had so many happy memories of this place! She and Stripe had become friends here while she healed his broken wing.

Twink's own wings felt leaden now as she thought of it. She had been so sure then that being a Fairy Medic was what she was meant to do. She'd never dreamed that she might not even pass her Creature Kindness practical.

'Hi,' said a voice. Glancing up, Twink saw Bimi hovering in the doorway. 'Are you OK?' her friend asked gently.

Twink tried to smile. Bimi swooped over and sat down beside her on the bed. Neither fairy spoke for a moment.

'Well . . . at least now we know that Horace Cloudwing was a total moss brain,' said Bimi finally, rubbing her wing against Twink's.

Laughter burst out of Twink despite herself. The more she laughed, the funnier it seemed. Bimi started laughing too, until suddenly the pair of them were lying back on the bed, kicking their heels.

'Yes!' gasped Twink. 'We should write and tell him so!'

'*Dear Mr Cloudwing – hazelnuts are rubbish!*' cried Bimi.

After a while their laughter faded, and the two girls lay quietly on the bed, side by side.

'Bimi, what will I do if I don't pass?' said Twink, staring at the ceiling. 'Being a Fairy Medic is all I've ever wanted to do.'

Bimi sighed. 'Oh, Twink . . . I really think you should talk to Mr Woodleaf. Maybe it's not as bad as you think.'

'It is, though – I should be doing a lot better than this!' Twink sat up. 'I can't let him know how rubbish I am, Bimi. I've *got* to find a way to make friends with the starling.'

There was silence for a moment. Bimi sat up as well, tracing a pattern on the worn petal duvet. 'Twink . . . can I tell you something?'

Twink's eyes widened. 'Of course! You can tell me anything, you know that.'

Taking a deep breath, Bimi blurted out, 'It's just that – well – I want to try to take advanced Creature Kindness next year, too.'

Twink gaped at her. 'You mean . . . *you* want to be a Fairy Medic?' she said in amazement.

Bimi's cheeks blazed red. 'I know I'm probably not clever enough. I – I've been studying on my own because I haven't wanted to tell anyone; I was afraid you'd all laugh . . .'

'Don't be daft!' cried Twink, nudging her. 'I just thought you wanted to be a model, that's all.' The term before, Bimi had been a huge hit in the Second Year's fairy fashion show, and Twink had assumed that her friend would want to continue modelling.

Bimi looked horrified. 'A *model*? The fashion show was just a bit of fun! No, I – I always sort of thought I'd like to be a Fairy Medic, but . . .' she trailed off.

Twink brushed her wing against Bimi's. 'Go on! What were you going to say?'

'I do so badly in exams, *that's* what.' Bimi scuffed at the floor with her toe. 'Twink, it's what I really, really want to do – but how will I ever score high enough in the written exam?'

So *that's* what had been bothering Bimi! 'By studying, that's how,' said Twink firmly. 'You'll be fine. You're a lot cleverer than you think you are, you know.'

Bimi made a face. 'Yes, right! My mind always turns to slush whenever I'm asked a question. How is that clever?'

'That's got nothing to *do* with being clever – it's just nerves,' said Twink. 'Bimi, listen! We've still got three weeks before the exams, so we'll study together for them. I'll make sure you know it all so well that your mind won't be *able* to turn to slush!'

A look of cautious hope appeared on Bimi's face. 'Do you really think so?'

'I *know* so,' promised Twink, squeezing her friend's hand. 'You'll pass the exam with flying colours, wait and see!'

* * *

That night Twink lay staring out of her window long after the rest of Peony Branch had fallen into slumbering silence. A light snowfall had begun. The flakes spiralled gently down like tiny pieces of lace.

Twink sighed. There was no uncertainty at all in her mind that *Bimi* could become a Fairy Medic . . . but for the first time ever, Twink's own future seemed full of doubt.

Chapter Six

'Let's try another one,' said Twink, flipping the page. 'What are the three ways you can cheer up a depressed frog?'

Bimi rubbed her temples. 'Depressed frogs, depressed frogs . . . oh, I've got it!' she cried. 'You can tickle their tummies, or sing to them, or – or give them a bath in sparkling dew.'

'Yes!' Twink beamed, and snapped the book shut. 'That's brilliant – you've hardly got anything wrong for days now!'

Bimi played with her blue second-year sash,

'Twink, do you *really* think I can do well in the exam?'

'I really do,' said Twink seriously. 'You know all of the material – you just have to keep calm, somehow.'

'Somehow.' Bimi grimaced.

The two friends were sitting in the second-year Common Branch, studying at adjoining mushroom desks. In past terms, the Common Branch had rung with chatter and laughter. This term, the only sound was the turning of pages, and the low murmur of fairies quizzing each other for their exams – now only a few days away.

Twink's wings felt icy at the thought. The Seedling Exams were really almost here, after a whole term of worrying about them! *By this time next week, I'll know whether I can be a Fairy Medic or not*, she thought. Her stomach knotted.

'Bimi, listen,' she whispered as an idea came to her. 'Before the exam starts, let's – let's look at each other and think encouraging thoughts, all right?'

Bimi blinked. 'What do you mean?'

Twink clutched her hand. 'Right before the exam starts, look over at me and think, *You can do it, Twink,* as hard as you can! And I'll be looking at you, thinking the same thing.' Suddenly she felt embarrassed. 'I don't know – it's probably a stupid idea . . .'

'No, it's not!' Bimi's blue eyes shone. 'Oh, Twink, I think it would really help to calm me down. Let's do it!'

They touched their wings in a promise. Bimi smiled ruefully. 'Besides . . . it's a lot better than my *other* idea.'

'What other idea?' Twink looked at her curiously.

Bimi's cheeks blazed. 'Well . . . I went into Mr Woodleaf's branch a few days ago to ask him something about my dormouse. He wasn't there, but one of his desk drawers was open, and – and I saw the answers to the exam in it.'

'Bimi!' gasped Twink in alarm. 'You didn't –'

'No,' said Bimi in a low voice. 'I was tempted, though!' She pulled her knees up to her chest and sighed. 'But then I thought, if the only way I can take the advanced classes is by cheating, then I don't deserve to be a Fairy Medic, do I?'

Twink squeezed her arm. 'You *do* deserve to be a Fairy Medic,' she said warmly. 'I'm glad you didn't look at the answers, Bimi – you'll do fine on your own, wait and see.'

Suddenly a prickly feeling darted across her wings, as if someone were watching them. Looking over her shoulder, Twink saw Mariella gazing down at her books. The pointy-faced fairy turned a page, looking utterly engrossed . . . but there was a faint spot of red on her cheeks.

Twink frowned uneasily. How much had Mariella heard?

Bang! The Common Branch jumped as Sooze slammed her book shut. 'Do you two *have* to be so loud?' she snapped at Sili and Zena. 'You're not the only ones trying to study, you know.'

A silence fell as everyone stared at her. 'What do you mean?' asked Zena in surprise. 'We're just going over the fairy dust spells – we weren't being any louder than anyone else.'

'Oh, just go somewhere else, will you?' groaned Sooze. 'I can hardly hear myself think!'

Sili's eyes flashed. 'We will not. We've as much right to be here as you.'

'Not if you're bothering the whole branch, you haven't!' retorted Sooze.

Kiki looked worried. '*I* didn't hear them,' she said. 'Sooze, I think maybe you're just worried about the exams –'

'Well, who asked *you*?' demanded Sooze. 'Just keep out of this, Kiki!'

Sili crossed her arms coldly over her chest. 'You know what, Sooze – everyone's been studying hard this term, but *you've* completely changed! You're no fun at all any more.'

'*Fun?*' Sooze leapt up from her desk, her fists clenched. For a moment Twink thought she was going to fly right at Sili and box her ears.

'*Fun?*' Sooze repeated. Her voice shook, and suddenly she looked close to tears. 'No – no, I don't suppose I am!' And she grabbed up her books and jetted out of the branch.

The second-year fairies glanced at each other. Pix sighed. 'She must be worried sick with the exams almost here. I know she was being unfair, Sili, but you shouldn't have told her off.'

'Me? She started it!' said Sili, flipping back her silver hair in exasperation. '*Everyone's* worried; it's no excuse for snarling at us.'

'I'm going after her,' whispered Twink to Bimi. Her friend nodded, and Twink skimmed out of the Common Branch.

It didn't take long to find Sooze. She was hovering beside a window on the other side of the trunk, with her hands over her face and her shoulders shaking. Twink flew across to her. 'Are you all right?'

Sooze's head jerked up. She wiped her eyes quickly, scowling. 'Fine!'

'Well, good,' said Twink, trying to smile. 'I just thought I'd check, that's all.'

There was a silence. Sooze glared out of the window, her chin stiff.

'But . . . you know,' went on Twink, 'if you *did* want to talk, or anything . . .'

Sooze's face seemed to crumple. 'Oh, Twink, I'm so scared! I've just *got* to do well in the exams.' There was a knobbly bit on the wall: a sort of window seat, set high over the school's floor. Sooze sank down on to it, biting her lip.

'I know,' murmured Twink, sitting down beside her. 'But, Sooze –'

'No, you *don't* know,' interrupted Sooze. 'My parents –' she gulped. 'Oh, Twink, they were so upset when they found out about the fairy dust flares! I've never seen them like that.'

Twink gently rubbed her friend's wing with her own. Sooze took a ragged breath. 'They were so – sad, and disappointed. They said that they blamed themselves, for not being firmer with me before. And – and that they knew I'd do my best, but they'd understand if I didn't move up to the third year with the rest of you . . .' Sooze trailed off.

Twink's eyebrows drew together in confusion. 'But – if they'd understand – '

Sooze spun sharply towards her. 'Don't you see?' she cried, her eyes bright. 'I *can't* let them down

again! I've *got* to do well enough in my exams to move up into the third year – or die trying!'

Sitting alone at her mushroom desk, Mariella gazed down at her books with a small, secret smile.

What fantastic luck to have overheard Bimi! She'd sneak down to Mr Woodleaf's branch and copy out the answers the first chance she got. It hardly even counted as cheating, either. She *would* have known all the answers, if she'd only had time to study. It wasn't her fault that she hadn't, with all those stupid practicals they'd been given!

It was true that the others had somehow squeezed in studying time this term, but Mariella had been too fed up with schoolwork to bother. Now, however, with the written exams only a few days away, it was a jolt to realise that she couldn't catch up as easily as she'd thought.

In fact . . . in fact, she was starting to feel a bit frightened whenever she thought about it. Mariella closed her Creature Kindness book. At least that was one exam taken care of! And the rest couldn't be *that* difficult. After all, the current batch of third-year students had got through them – and they were all total wasp brains!

Chapter
Seven

All too soon, the day of the first written exam arrived. After breakfast that morning, Twink sat with the other second-year students in the Great Branch. The rest of the school had departed for lessons, leaving the Second Years to hear an announcement from Miss Sparkle.

It's just like the meeting at the start of term, thought Twink. Except that they'd all been through so much now! The students who gazed back at Miss Sparkle were all a bit older and wiser than they'd been before.

'You've been studying hard, and you should be very proud of yourselves,' said their year head warmly. 'The first exams are scheduled for this afternoon after lunch. I've posted the timetable just outside the Great Branch.'

Twink glanced at the closed doors. From the pale faces around her, she knew that the others were dying to get to the timetable as badly as she was.

Miss Sparkle continued. 'You all have the morning off, and I suggest that you spend it doing anything *except* studying! Go for a long flight and clear your head a bit; it'll do you good. Go on, now – and good luck!'

With murmured thanks the second-year fairies skimmed rapidly from the Great Branch. The timetable was on a large oak leaf that hung on the wall. The fairies hovered before it in an anxious cluster, jostling to see.

'Peony Branch has got Creature Kindness for the first written exam,' called down Pix, who had shot above the others for a better look. 'Then tomorrow morning we've got the Flower Power exam, with the

Creature Kindness practical right after it. Weather Magic is tomorrow afternoon . . .'

Twink's heart sank as she caught a glimpse of the oak leaf. Pix was right: their Creature Kindness practical was the very next morning. She had hoped to have a few more days with the bird, to have a last chance at making him like her – but instead there was no time at all!

The red-haired fairy swooped back to where the others were hovering. 'I'm going to study some more,' she said flatly. 'I don't care what Miss Sparkle thinks – *she's* not the one who has to take the exams!' She jetted off towards the Common Branch.

'Me too,' mumbled Sooze, looking pale. 'I – I just need to go over a few things.'

Twink watched sympathetically as her friend flitted off. It would be such a relief for Sooze when the exams were over!

'Well, I think a break's a good idea,' said Zena, bobbing in the air. 'I'm going to fly down to the Dingly Dell – would anyone like to come?'

Several fairies chorused agreement. 'Ooh, yes,

please!' cried Kiki, clapping her hands. 'I've still not seen it.'

'Yes, I'll come,' said Mariella. She tossed back her silvery-green hair with a smug smile. 'I'm not worried about *this* exam.'

'Are you going?' whispered Twink to Bimi. Her friend shook her head. 'No, I – I think I'll study a bit more, too. What about you?'

Twink hesitated. Regardless of Miss Sparkle's advice, she thought that more studying might be a good idea. She was going to have to do extremely well in her written Creature Kindness exam to make up for her practical!

Making up her mind, Twink shook her head. 'No, I'm going to go down to the animal infirmary. I want to try one last time to win over my starling.'

Bimi nodded. 'All right – good luck!' Suddenly the pretty fairy squeezed Twink's hand.

'Oh, Twink, I'm so nervous!' she breathed. 'If I didn't know that you're going to be right there with me before the exam, thinking *You can do it, Bimi* – then I don't think I could face it at all!'

* * *

Twink flew slowly down to the hollow log, thinking of her friends. Everyone had worked so hard this term! *Oh, I hope we all do well,* she thought, entering the warm log and shutting the door behind her. It would be awful if the Peony Branch fairies were separated.

Then she grimaced. Well – she could probably live without Mariella moving up with them, if she had to!

Skimming past the other animals, Twink put a welcoming smile on her face. 'Hello!' she said as she rounded the corner of the alcove. 'How are . . .'

Her voice petered off as she stared at the empty nest. The starling was gone.

Twink's thoughts whirled in confusion. Had the bird's wing finally healed, and Mr Woodleaf forgotten to tell her? No, that was impossible – he'd said that they had their animals until the end of term!

Besides, now that she looked, she could see that the water bucket beside the bird's nest had been overturned. Damp footprints hopped their way across the wooden floor. Twink's heart thudded as she noticed that the back door had been forced open, with harsh peck-marks gouging the wood.

Suddenly Mr Woodleaf's words came back to her: *They hate being cooped up ... they've even been known to try to leave before they can fly again.*

Oh, this was all her fault! Twink felt the blood leave her face. Mr Woodleaf had told her that she'd have to work hard to keep the bird's mind off things – if she'd managed to make friends with him, this never would have happened!

She jetted out of the door and hovered, staring wildly around her. Which way had he headed? The answer came to her instantly. He spent all his time staring longingly out of the window at the wood – of course that's where he'd gone!

If only the snow hadn't melted, Twink thought as she skimmed towards the woods. Then she could just follow his tracks and have him back in no time! But the weather had turned warmer over the last few days, taking the snow with it.

Reaching the forest, Twink hovered at the treeline, gazing helplessly around her. Where to even begin?

Hang on – maybe one of the dryads had seen him! Flying hastily to the young birch tree, Twink settled herself under it. *Sheena, it's me! I need your help!*

The tall, snowy-white girl appeared instantly. *Twink! What's wrong?*

Quickly Twink explained, her words tumbling over each other. *Have you seen him?* she finished urgently. *He still can't fly; he's in danger!*

Sheena shook her head. *No, he didn't pass by me. But Twink, you can't go around asking every dryad – it'll take you ages!*

Remembering her search for the hazel tree, Twink knew Sheena was right. *But what can I do?* she implored. *I have to find him!*

Sheena hesitated. *Well . . . there is one thing . . . but I don't know if it will work. You could try to contact the spirit of the wood.*

The spirit of the wood? repeated Twink in bewilderment. She hadn't even known there was such a thing!

Sheena nodded. *Every wood has an overall spirit: like a dryad, but much more powerful. She can be contacted if you try hard enough. But* . . . she stopped, furrowing her brow.

What? asked Twink. Her heart felt like a woodpecker hammering in her chest.

Well . . . *I've never heard of a fairy as young as you doing it,* admitted Sheena. *Usually it's a group of older fairies, and even then it sometimes doesn't work.*

Disappointment crashed over Twink. Oh, it sounded impossible! If older fairies couldn't manage it, then how could *she* hope to, when she was only a second-year student?

Then she thought of the starling, dragging his broken wing behind him . . . and she took a deep breath. *I've still got to try,* she said firmly. *Can you tell me what to do?*

Twink stood in the forest clearing, trying not to think about how much time had already passed. Why hadn't she dashed back to school and got help the moment she saw the bird was missing? Dozens of fairies together could have branched out through the wood and found him in no time!

But she hadn't. And now almost an hour had gone by, and she seemed no closer to contacting the spirit of the wood than before. *I'll try one last time,* thought Twink wretchedly. *Then I'll have to go and get help.*

Taking a deep breath, she closed her eyes and tried to imagine the entire wood, as Sheena had instructed her: all of the roots, the hundreds of tree trunks, the thousands of branches stretching towards the sky. And the woodland creatures, too: its rabbits and birds, its insects, the fish swimming in its brook.

Finally, Twink reached out with her mind. *Spirit of the wood, are you there? Please answer me . . . I'm trying to find an injured starling. I have to save him!*

She stood as still as she could, hardly daring to breathe. The minutes passed. Then, when Twink had almost given up hope, she felt it: a faint rustling deep within her, like a hundred trees softly sighing.

She caught her breath. *Spirit? Is that you?*

The sensation faded. There was only the cold clearing, and a few stray snowflakes starting to fall.

Twink's shoulders slumped. She had only imagined it. Oh, how stupid she had been, to think that she could contact the spirit of the wood on her own! And now precious time had been wasted. *Anything* could have happened to the starling.

Dejectedly, Twink turned and started to fly back to school for help.

'Caw!'

She started and looked up. A crow was sitting in a nearby pine tree, watching her. When he saw that he had her attention, he flew a few trees away, and then called again.

It's almost as if he wants me to follow him, thought Twink in surprise. But she didn't have time; she had to find the starling!

The crow hopped up and down on his branch. There was an urgent look in his bright, black eyes.

'Do – do you know where the starling is?' asked Twink hesitantly, flitting towards him.

'Caw!' The crow flapped his dark wings.

'All right, then!' decided Twink suddenly. 'I'll follow you.'

The crow led her deep into the wood, winging his way from branch to branch – but always stopping just ahead of her, making sure that she was following. Finally, when Twink had started to think he didn't know anything after all, he swooped down towards a small clearing and pointed with his wing.

'Caw!' he said.

Twink gasped. There below was the starling,

struggling through the undergrowth with his broken wing – with a blaze of red and white creeping just after him. A fox!

'No!' cried Twink. Without thinking, she darted down just as the fox was ready to pounce. 'Get off him!' she shrieked, swatting at the fox's nose.

The fox blinked and backed away a step. Then he saw how small his attacker was, and his golden eyes narrowed. Twink gulped, and somersaulted out of his way just as he lunged at her. Foxes were usually friendly to fairies – but this one was obviously hungry!

The fox leapt at the starling again, his sharp teeth glinting. '*No!*' shouted Twink.

She grabbed the fox's long tail and tugged hard. The fox growled, whirling about and snapping at her. Twink hastily let go, and found herself tumbling through the air like a leaf in a storm.

'Eek!' she shrieked, struggling to right herself.

When the world was right-side up again, Twink shook her head in a daze. On the other side of the clearing, the starling was trying to hide under a

fallen log. The fox grinned, ready to jump.

'Stop!' cried Twink, close to tears. She was too far away now to do any good, but she aimed herself at the fox anyway, gritting her teeth as she flew as fast as she could.

All at once a large black bird came screaming down from the sky. The crow hovered in front of the fox, cawing and flapping its wings. The fox yelped in alarm – and then turned and ran, padding away into the forest.

'Oh, thank you!' gasped Twink. 'Thank you!' But the crow was already gone, flying silently through the trees.

Twink jetted to the fallen log and peered under it. The starling sat huddled in the shadows, breathing hard.

'It's OK,' said Twink gently. 'The fox is gone.'

The bird ruffled up his feathers without looking at her. He seemed utterly miserable.

Twink stared at him in a conflict of emotions. She didn't like him, she realised suddenly. She had never liked him, not from the start. But it was impossible

not to feel sorry for him, crouched there with his grimy feathers sticking out.

Twink swallowed hard as something else occurred to her. Why had she expected to win him over, when she didn't care about him? She had only ever cared about passing her practical! No wonder the starling had never warmed to her – he had seen right through her.

Twink reached out her hand to him. 'Come on,' she said softly. 'I – I know we're not friends, but you can't stay here. I'll take you back to the infirmary.'

The starling seemed subdued as Twink helped him back into his nest. She gave him some seeds and water, and when he had finished he sighed tiredly, closing his eyes. Soon his snores were filling the room.

Twink put the buckets away, and mended the back door as best she could – though somehow, she didn't think the bird would try to escape again. The long journey through the wood and over the field had obviously exhausted him.

For a moment, Twink stood watching the starling as he slept. She smiled sadly. Maybe, if they had had just a bit more time together, they could have become friends after all. But with the practical tomorrow, there didn't seem much hope now.

A sudden thought struck Twink like lightning. *Her exam!* Glancing out of the window at the sun, her wings froze with horror.

Her Creature Kindness exam had begun five minutes ago.

Chapter Eight

Red-faced and panting, Twink jetted into the Creature Kindness branch. Everyone was already hard at work, with their heads bowed over their exam petals. The only sound was the scratching of snail-trail pens.

Mr Woodleaf looked up in surprise. 'Twink!' he whispered. 'You're late.'

'I'm sorry,' mumbled Twink, her ears burning.

She flitted to the only empty mushroom left, at the back of the branch. Remembering her pact with Bimi, she glanced quickly up, hoping to catch her

friend's eye – but from where she sat, she could only see the back of Bimi's dark blue head.

Tears pricked at Twink's eyes. Oh, it was all going wrong! How could she ever forgive herself for letting Bimi down?

Mr Woodleaf placed an exam petal on her desk, and she fumbled in her bag for her snail-trail pen. She quickly wrote her name at the top, trying to calm down.

Sitting beside her, Mariella was frowning, flipping through her exam petal by petal. 'But this is the wrong one!' she cried suddenly.

Mr Woodleaf gave her a considering look. 'Were you expecting a different exam, Mariella?' he asked pointedly.

Her cheeks flushed. 'No, sir,' she muttered.

Glancing at her, Twink thought that Mariella looked quite ill, but she had no time to dwell on it. *Never mind*, she thought fervently. Bimi knows I'm wishing her well, and I know she's doing the same for me!

Twink took a deep breath, her fingers tightening around her pen – and began.

* * *

'At first it was awful,' admitted Bimi as they sat chatting on her bed later that afternoon. 'When I saw you still weren't back, I started to panic! But then I looked at the questions, and I thought, *I know that one*. So I wrote down the answer, and then I saw that I knew the next one, too –'

'Oh, Bimi, that's wonderful!' cried Twink, clutching her friend's arm. 'I *knew* you could do it!'

'Don't get too excited yet,' said Bimi with a sigh. 'There was a lot I wasn't sure about. Anyway, how do you think *you* did?'

'I don't know,' said Twink, her jubilation fading. 'I was so flustered when I first flew in, I could hardly think.' Her wings went clammy as she thought of it. Names and remedies had swirled about in her head like a snowstorm – and whether they had landed in the right places or not, she had no idea.

'Well, there's still the practical,' said Bimi after a pause.

Twink tried to smile. 'I don't think I'll do very well in it, though. I – I suppose I'll just have to see what happens.'

Their Flower Power exam the next morning seemed simple in comparison. Twink wrote her answers quickly, losing herself in the world of trees and plants. She completed her last question just as the magpie's call sounded through the school, and sighed with relief as she put her pen down.

'Just a moment before you leave, class,' said Miss

Petal. 'I know this may seem strange, but – did anyone here contact the spirit of the wood yesterday morning?'

Twink sat up in alarm. Her friends shook their heads, glancing blankly at each other.

'But that's quite an advanced spell, isn't it, Miss Petal?' said Pix with a frown.

Their Flower Power teacher nodded, shuffling the exam petals together. 'Yes, that's why I'm curious. A few of the dryads were talking about it yesterday, when the Marigold Branch fairies were doing their practicals. I suppose it must have been one of the upper-year fairies.'

'*I'm* not so sure of that,' said Sooze, raising a lavender eyebrow. 'Do you want to confess anything, Opposite?'

Twink's pointed ears burned. Naturally, the whole branch knew by now how skilled she was at talking to dryads! 'Um . . . well, I tried, but I didn't manage to do it,' she mumbled.

Miss Petal's eyes widened. 'Really? Stay behind, Twink. I want to talk to you for a moment.'

When the others had left, Miss Petal sat perched on her mushroom desk, folding her wings behind her back. 'Now, then – tell me everything!' she said with a smile.

Twink took a deep breath. The story came spilling out: how she had become friends with Sheena and the other dryads, how she had roused the ancient hazel dryad . . . and finally, how she had tried and failed to reach the spirit of the wood.

'I know it was stupid of me even to try,' she finished, her cheeks hot with embarrassment. 'Sheena *told* me I was too young, but I didn't listen.'

Miss Petal shook her head. 'No, Twink, I think you *did* reach the spirit of the wood. She often works through other creatures, you know. I'm sure that's why the crow suddenly came to help you.'

'Oh!' gasped Twink. Her hands flew to her mouth as the puzzle pieces fell into place. 'I never thought of that!'

Miss Petal smiled at her expression. 'You seem to have quite a talent for working with trees, Twink. Have you considered taking the advanced Flower

Power classes next year?'

Advanced *Flower Power*?

'No,' said Twink, too startled to be polite. 'I want to take advanced Creature Kindness, so I can be a Fairy Medic like my parents.'

'Well, you'll obviously pass your Flower Power practical with full marks,' said Miss Petal. 'And I was watching you during the exam this morning; I'd be surprised if you had any trouble with it.'

'No, I – I think I probably did pretty well,' Twink admitted. 'But –' She fell silent, confused by her whirlwind of thoughts. She had *always* wanted to be a Fairy Medic, from the time she was a tiny little fairy. How could she change her dream now?

But . . . talking with dryads was so glimmery . . . and she had actually reached the spirit of the wood!

Miss Petal slid off her desk. 'Just think about it, Twink,' she said gently. 'It would be a shame to waste such a talent. You could always take both of them – as you've already seen, you can combine Flower Power with Creature Kindness to great effect.'

With a final smile, Miss Petal flitted out of the branch, leaving Twink on her own. 'Flower Power,' she murmured. Unexpectedly, a rustle of excitement darted across her wings.

Then her face fell. Glumly, she picked up her petal bag. It was all very well to talk about taking both of them – but she'd be lucky now if she got to take advanced Creature Kindness at all.

Later that morning the Peony Branch fairies stood waiting in the animal infirmary for Mr Woodleaf to arrive. Looking around, Twink saw that her friends had all made a special effort for the practical: Bimi had combed her dormouse's fur until it shone, and tied a jaunty blue ribbon around his tail. Sooze's cricket wore a red bow tie. Even Mariella had made a last-minute attempt, tying a drooping pink ribbon around her rat's middle.

Twink sighed as she glanced at the starling. His speckled feathers were as grimy as ever, and he had a cross look on his face. It was obvious that the two of them didn't get on, thought Twink sadly – but there wasn't anything she could do about it now.

Mr Woodleaf flitted in, clover-leaf pad in hand. 'Good, you're all here!' he said cheerfully. 'Who'd like to go first?'

Twink raised her hand. 'I will,' she said. She might as well get it over with.

As Mr Woodleaf watched, she fed and watered the starling, standing well back so that he couldn't swipe her with his wing. But to her surprise, he didn't even try. He nibbled his seeds docilely, and blinked at her once he'd finished.

Confused, Twink carefully changed his bandage, wrapping the leafy strips around his injured wing. The bird ruffled his feathers – but for the first time, it seemed an ordinary gesture rather than an angry one. *What* was going on?

Twink turned to Mr Woodleaf. 'That's, um . . . all,' she said. 'He won't let me groom him.'

'Excellent,' said Mr Woodleaf, writing something on his clover pad. 'You've done a very good job.'

Twink's mouth dropped open. 'I have?'

Mr Woodleaf's green eyebrows rose in surprise.

'Yes, of course. Even better than I thought you would, in fact.'

Twink's head spun. 'But – but I don't understand,' she stammered. 'You said we had to work well with our animal, and I *haven't* – we don't like each other, we never have! And – and he ran away yesterday, and I had to go and find him –'

Mr Woodleaf shook his head. 'Working well with an animal doesn't always mean you become friends with it, Twink. Starlings are difficult birds – you've done well just by being patient with him.' He smiled suddenly. 'Besides, I'm not sure you're right that he doesn't like you. He looks friendlier now than I've ever seen him!'

Twink stared at the starling. He gazed complacently back at her.

Mr Woodleaf was right, she thought in a daze. What on earth had happened? Was it because she'd saved him from the fox? Or simply that, for the first time, she'd been honest with him about her feelings?

Whatever it was . . . the two of them had somehow found a way to get on.

Mr Woodleaf patted her on the shoulder and flitted across to the next student. Not taking her eyes off the starling, Twink moved forward until she stood just beside him. Suddenly there was so much she wanted to say that words seemed useless.

'Thank you for letting me take care of you,' she said softly. 'I'll come back and see you again soon, before the end of term.'

Very, very slowly, she reached out and stroked his good wing, feeling the sleek smoothness of his brown feathers. With a sigh, the starling closed his eyes and seemed to smile.

The rest of the exams passed in a blur of test questions and practicals. Twink produced a passable flower dress, and performed the pleasant dreams dance almost perfectly. And in Weather Magic, her snowflakes flurried just as they were supposed to – though the written exam turned out to be much more difficult than she had expected!

And then all at once, the exams were over.

The night before the last day of term, Twink and

her friends packed their oak-leaf bags in silence. Their results would be displayed outside the Great Branch first thing the next morning, and then their parents would be arriving to take them home after breakfast.

On the whole, Twink thought she had done well . . . except for her awful Creature Kindness exam, when she had been too panicked to think. A sick feeling clutched her stomach whenever she thought of it.

Twink tucked a spare pair of pixie boots into her bag. Still, she was glad that she had gone to find the starling that morning – even if it meant she had messed up her chance of being a Fairy Medic for ever.

Finally Twink closed her bag and fastened its bark catch. 'Well . . . goodbye, Peony Branch,' she said, looking around her. She thought the bright pink peonies that hung over each bed looked sad, as if they knew the fairies were leaving.

'Oh, stop!' cried Sili. 'I'm feeling all sad now.'

'I know,' said Pix, swallowing hard. 'I'm really

going to miss it here.'

'Pillow fight!' screeched Sooze suddenly. Flitting up to the ceiling, she flung her pillow at Kiki's curly head.

Instantly, chaos erupted through Peony Branch. The fairies darted about the room, hurling pillows and screaming with laughter. Twink shrieked as one came hurtling towards her, and did a quick midair somersault to get away.

'Take that!' she shouted, snatching the pillow up and throwing it back at Zena. Oh, it felt so wonderful to laugh again after the pressure of the exams!

But no one was laughing the next morning as they flew down to the Great Branch. Twink and Bimi clutched hands as they spiralled downwards. Bimi looked ghostly-pale. Twink didn't blame her. She felt almost dizzy with nerves herself.

A cold hand slipped into her free one. 'Do you mind, Opposite?' whispered Sooze. 'I – I'm feeling sort of nervous.'

Twink squeezed her friend's hand. They arrived at

the Great Branch, and hesitated. Other second-year fairies were already there, either shrieking exultantly or turning away wretched-faced.

'Well – here goes,' murmured Twink. Sooze nodded, wide-eyed. Bimi gulped, and nodded too. The three of them flew forward.

At first Twink couldn't find her name. She skimmed the leaf wildly, her heart thumping. Then all at once it jumped out at her: *Twink Flutterby: 427 points. Creature Kindness: 86. Flower Power: 92. Weather Magic: 79 . . .*

Twink's shoulders sagged in relief. She had done it. Oh, even with her awful Creature Kindness exam, she had somehow done it!

'Twink . . . look,' choked out Bimi, her eyes bright with tears. Glancing quickly at her friend, Twink searched for Bimi's name, dreading what she might see.

Bimi Bluebell: 392 points. Creature Kindness: 89. Flower Power . . .

'Bimi!' shrieked Twink, throwing her arms around her neck. 'You did it! You really did it!' The two

fairies bobbed in the air together, hugging hard.

'I can't believe it, I can't believe it!' gasped Bimi.

Suddenly a piercing scream echoed through the tree trunk. 'I DID IT!' whooped Sooze, punching the air and doing a back flip. 'I DID IT! I DID IT!' She flung herself at Twink and Bimi. The three fairies' wings fluttered madly as they clutched at each other, screaming and laughing.

'*I'll* say you did, Sooze,' breathed Zena, looking at the results. 'You came fifth in our whole year, even

with failing your Fairy Dust practical!'

'And Pix came first, of course!' teased Sili, tugging the red-haired fairy's cap down.

Pix's eyes were shining, but she looked limp with relief. 'They were a lot harder than I thought they'd be,' she admitted. 'Oh, I can't believe I really came first! My parents are going to be thrilled.'

With a rustle of white wings, Miss Sparkle arrived. 'Well done, girls!' she beamed. 'You've all done brilliantly – and you especially, Sooze. I knew you could do it, my dear.'

Sooze flushed bright red. 'I wasn't sure at all,' she confessed. 'But I'm so glad I did!'

Miss Sparkle smiled warmly at her. 'You've the makings of a fine fairy, Sooze – maybe now you'll start to take yourself a bit more seriously.' She glanced around the group. 'Mariella, may I have a word? We have a few things to discuss.'

Suddenly Twink noticed how sick and pale Mariella looked. Miss Sparkle flew the pointy-faced fairy a little distance away from the others, talking earnestly to her. Mariella stared down at the ground, mumbling her replies.

Frowning, Twink looked at the results again – and gasped. 'Oh, no! Look at Mariella's scores.'

The others gazed at Mariella's results in stunned silence. 'Oh, Mosquito Nose!' groaned Sooze, slapping her forehead. 'You silly fairy – you didn't study at all, did you?'

Mariella Gossamer: 295 points. Creature Kindness: 55. Flower Power: 47. Dance: 43 . . . the numbers marched on, each more awful than the last.

Twink swallowed hard as she remembered Mariella during the Creature Kindness exam. 'I – I think she tried to cheat in Creature Kindness,' she said in a low voice.

'Well, it serves her right, I suppose,' said Sooze, shaking her head. 'But it's not going to be the same, moving up to Third Year without old Mosquito Nose – and I never thought I'd say that!'

As the Peony Branch fairies watched, Miss Sparkle patted Mariella's shoulder and flew off. Mariella hovered listlessly where she was, gazing at her pixie boots.

'Wasps – she must feel awful!' muttered Sooze. She hesitated, fluttering her pink wings. Then all at once she skimmed across to Mariella. A moment later, she had her arm around Mariella's shoulders, talking softly to her.

The Peony Branch fairies looked at each other.

'Come on,' said Twink suddenly.

As one, she and her friends flew over to join them, hovering around Mariella in a bright rainbow of wings. The pointy-faced fairy wiped her eyes and tried to laugh. 'Oh, no! Not more of you. Does *everyone* know?'

'Are you OK?' asked Bimi, touching her arm.

Mariella sighed. 'My father's going to *kill* me when he finds out I tried to cheat, not to mention failing my exams.' She took a deep breath. 'But Miss Sparkle said she'd talk to him about special classes for me over the hols, so . . .' she trailed off.

'Good!' said Pix. 'You could do really well if you tried, Mariella.'

Mariella shrugged her lacy green wings glumly. 'I don't know if I'll do well enough to move up, though. There's so much to catch up on!'

Sooze shook her shoulders. 'Of course you can! Look at me – who would have thought that *I* could ever come fifth in the whole year?'

'Well, there is that,' said Mariella with a tiny smile.

The magpie's call echoed through the school. 'Come on – it's time for breakfast,' said Zena. 'Then our parents will be here!'

As the Peony Branch fairies flew towards the Great Branch, Twink looked at the oak-leaf notice again and smiled. *I'm so lucky!* she thought. She had her old dream of becoming a Fairy Medic – and now a new dream, too. She'd take the advanced Flower Power classes next year as Miss Petal had suggested, and see where they led her.

Bimi, as she so often did, seemed to read Twink's thoughts. 'Would your parents mind if you became a Wood Guardian instead of a Fairy Medic?' she whispered, linking her arm through Twink's.

Twink shrugged. 'They might be a little disap-pointed – but I think they just want me to be happy. Besides, I haven't decided anything yet,' she added with a grin. 'I just have more choices now, that's all!'

And it was true. Maybe she'd be a Fairy Medic who talked with the dryads – or maybe she'd end up working with trees and forests. Who knew? It all seemed terribly exciting!

Sooze linked arms with Twink on the other side. 'It's our last breakfast as Second Years!' she cried as they flew into the Great Branch. Laughing, the other Peony Branch fairies linked on as well, so that all at once they were flying in a long, wavering line.

Afterwards, Twink wasn't sure who it was who started to sing, but soon all the fairies in the school were joining in – even Miss Shimmery and all their teachers, their voices echoing up to the rafters:

> *Oh, Glitterwings, dear Glitterwings*
> *Beloved oak tree scho-ool.*
> *Good fairy fun for everyone,*
> *That is our fairy ru-ule.*
> *Our teachers wise,*

Their magic strong.
With all our friends,
We can't go wrong.
Oh, Glitterwings, dear Glitterwings,
Beloved oak tree scho-ool!

Goodbye for now, Glitterwings, thought Twink
happily, squeezing the arms of her friends on either
side. *See you next year!*

Look out for a
special Christmas
Glitterwings
adventure!